Hello
Good Buy

Written by Dan Meyer

Illustrated by Crina Magalio

Hello Good Buy

On Super Bowl Sunday, five-year-old Steven
Johnson goes to the supermarket with his father.
Steven buys his favorite snack, jello.

This snack, however, is a new
brand and this jello talks!

Steven and his parents are in for a real battle,
as the jello tries to ruin their chance
to watch the Super Bowl. But Steven brilliantly
deals with his nemesis,
making a new friend in the process.

Copyright © 2020 by Dan Meyer
ISBN 978-1-71694-569-4
Imprint: Lulu.com

Super Bowl Sunday had finally arrived!
Five-year-old Steven Johnson was all excited as he put
on his Las Vegas Raiders uniform. Before the game,
he and his father would do some food shopping.

And so, they drove to the local supermarket.
While Mr. Johnson bought pretzels and tortilla chips,
Steven headed for his favorite snack, jello.
But something was different about the jello aisle today.
There was a new brand,
the Hello Yellow Jello Company.

Since Steven had always enjoyed trying new foods, he reached for the Hello Yellow Jello. As he grabbed the box, the most unusual thing happened...

"I'm magic and tragic!" exclaimed the box.

Steven was shocked by what he had heard, but he certainly didn't believe in talking jello. He kept the Hello Yellow Jello and proceeded to find his father. They paid for their snacks and returned home.

Steven's mother helped him make the Hello Yellow Jello.
"I see you found a new kind," said Mrs. Johnson.
"Yes," answered Steven, "The Hello Yellow Jello
Company jello should be great!"

Steven poured the contents of the package into a bowl.
Then Mrs. Johnson poured a cup of boiling
water over the yellow powder.

"Ouch!" responded the contents in the bowl.

Steven and his mother both looked at each other with
amazement, but like Steven, Mrs. Johnson
certainly didn't believe in talking jello either.

And so, Steven stirred the concoction
until it was completely dissolved. Then he added a cup
of cold water and continued to stir.
Finally, it was time to refrigerate the Hello Yellow Jello.

Steven and his parents then watched hours and hours of the Super Bowl Pregame show. They learned every little detail about the game.

The biggest thrill for Steven was
a commercial about – you guessed it –
the Hello Yellow Jello Company!

He ran back to the kitchen, opened the refrigerator door, and then shouted to his parents,

"Mom, Dad,
the Hello Yellow Jello is ready!"

Mrs. Johnson told Steven that he would have
to wait until after dinner to eat the Hello Yello Jello.

The family devoured a chicken with
vegetable stew meal, and now it was time
for the Hello Yellow Jello.

Steven's parents walked out of the kitchen and
put the football coverage back on the T.V.

Steven took the bowl of Hello Yellow Jello out
of the refrigerator, and then suddenly,
before you could say Hello Yellow Jello,
the mass of Hello Yellow Jello slid out of the bowl
and onto the floor.

A voice shouted, "I told you, I'm magic and tragic!"

Steven looked down at the Hello Yellow Jello.
It spoke again!

"I'm magic and tragic! Did you really think that you'd be able to eat me?"

"Get back into my bowl!" insisted Steven.
But the Hello Yellow Jello was not about to cooperate.

"You'll never get me. I'm going to
do the Hello Yellow Jello jiggle!"

And with that the Hello Yellow Jello
quickly jiggled all around Steven's feet.

The more Steven tried to corral this
slippery slitherer, the more frustrated he became.

The Hello Yellow Jello then slid its way into
the T.V. room. Before you could say
– that's right, Hello Yellow Jello – the creature
spread itself out and covered the T.V. screen.

"What's going on here?" yelled a shocked Mr. Johnson.

"What ever happened to that Hello Yellow Jello?" questioned Mrs. Johnson.

Everyone was quite upset, and the football game was about to start. The Hello Yellow Jello was basically glued to the T.V. screen.

Desperate for a solution to the problem, Steven pleaded with the Hello Yellow Jello.

"I promise I won't eat you," he stated.
And then he came up with a brilliant idea.

"Listen, Hello Yellow Jello. If you let us watch the Super Bowl, you'll see something about you!"

"All about me?" asked the Hello Yellow Jello.

"That's right," said Steven, "It will be special!"

The Hello Yellow Jello removed itself from the T.V. and sat down on the couch next to Steven.

The football game started and the Las Vegas Raiders scored right away. The first commercial break featured the Hello Yellow Jello Company.

And, of course,
the Hello Yellow Jello was overjoyed!

At halftime, the Las Vegas Raiders were way ahead! But Steven noticed that the Hello Yellow Jello was starting to lose its firm shape.

"I'd better get you back in the bowl and into the refrigerator. Then you'll be able to live forever!" Steven declared.

The Hello Yellow Jello thanked Steven for his concern, got back into the bowl, and shouted, "Let's go!"

The Las Vegas Raiders won the game, and Steven and his parents all agreed - it was a Hello Good Buy!